Also by Nick Butterworth

One Snowy Night
Just Like Jasper

With Mick Inkpen

The Nativity Play
Nice or Nasty

First U.S. Edition
ISBN 0-316-11919-9
Library of Congress Catalog Card Number 91-58568
Library of Congress Cataloging-in-Publication information is available.
10 9 8 7 6 5 4 3 2 1

Published simultaneously in Canada by Little, Brown & Company (Canada) Limited

Printed in Great Britain

ONE BLOWY NIGHT

NICK BUTTERWORTH

LITTLE, BROWN AND COMPANY
BOSTON TORONTO LONDON

Percy the park keeper couldn't sleep. Outside his hut a great storm was raging, with thunder and lightning and pouring rain.

Percy wasn't frightened by the thunder, and he loved to watch the lightning as it lit up the whole park. He didn't even mind the rain.

But there was one thing that Percy didn't like.

He didn't like the wind!
It blew down fences in the park and ripped branches off the trees. He didn't like it one bit.

"Oh, dear," he sighed as he watched from his window. The wind tugged at the trees, making them creak and groan. "It looks as if I'm going to be busy tomorrow."

He pulled his pillow over his head and tried to get to sleep.

Percy was up early in the morning. The wind had stopped and the sky was clear.

Percy loaded up his wheelbarrow with all the things he would need to make repairs and clean up after the storm. Then he set off to inspect the damage.

H e felt happy as he took deep breaths
of the fresh, clean air. Perhaps the
damage wouldn't be too bad.

But he was wrong. Something dreadful had happened. A great big oak tree that had stood by itself on the top of a little hill had been blown over by the storm.

The giant tree had been one of Percy's favorites. Now it looked very sad lying on its side with its mass of tangly roots sticking up into the air.

But it wasn't just one of *Percy's* favorite trees. Some of Percy's animal friends lived there. Now their homes were wrecked. Percy hurried up to the fallen tree.

The animals were gathered by the tree looking unhappy. When they saw Percy, everyone started talking at once.

Percy sat down with his friends and listened as they told how the storm had brought down the great tree.

"And now we have nowhere to live," said the badger. "Some of us lived in the tree, and some of us lived under it. But we're all homeless now."

Some of the rabbits looked close to tears, and the fox was sniffly. Percy passed him his handkerchief, and the fox blew his nose.

Percy stood up.

"We'll just have to find you somewhere else to live," he said. "Come on, everybody. Jump into my wheelbarrow." The animals felt better now that Percy was with them.

First he took them to the pine wood. But nobody wanted to live there.

"Too dark," squeaked the mice.

"Too gloomy," said the hedgehog.

So Percy took them to the shrubbery. But nobody wanted to live in the shrubbery either.

"No big trees," complained the squirrels.

"No big roots," moaned the rabbits.

"Never mind," said Percy. "We'll try across the stream."

Percy began to push the heavy wheelbarrow over a little bridge that crossed the stream. But as he got to the middle of the bridge, two things happened.

ercy stumbled— and the wheelbarrow
went directly into the water. SPLASH!

Suddenly Percy and his friends found
themselves drifting downstream to
where the stream opened out into a lake.

Percy stood up and looked around.

"We'll have to paddle ourselves to the shore,"
he said. But then something caught his eye.

"No, wait," said Percy. "Let's paddle across
to the other side of the lake. I have an idea."

The animals looked puzzled.

What was Percy up to? Slowly they
paddled the wheelbarrow across
to the distant shore.

Here we are!" said Percy.
The squirrels jumped ashore and
tied up the wheelbarrow to the roots of
an enormous hollow tree that grew by
the water's edge.

"Now, this is my plan," said Percy.
Everyone gathered round as Percy
explained his idea.

"Is everybody clear?"
Everyone nodded.
"Then let's get
to work!"

They began by unloading all Percy's tools and the planks of wood from the wheelbarrow. Then Percy explained exactly what he wanted each one to do.

He showed the badger how to use a saw, and he showed the squirrels how to hammer in nails. The fox drilled holes, and the rabbits screwed in screws. The mice were kept busy fetching and carrying for everyone else.

At lunchtime they took a short break to share some of Percy's peanut butter sandwiches. Then they got busy again.

At long last their work was finished. A very tired Percy stood back to admire their handiwork.

Now the squirrels had a brand-new home . . .

and so did the mice.

The rabbits had a new home . . .

and so did the badger.

And the fox.

And the hedgehog.

In fact, every one of Percy's friends
had a fine new place to live.

W ell done, everybody!" said Percy. "This is the best tree house I've ever seen!"

"What about you, Percy?" called the badger. "Aren't you going to join us?"

Percy smiled.

"I think I'll stick to my old hut," he said.

"Besides," said Percy, taking an acorn out of his pocket, "I still have one job left to do back at the little hill!"